ALLERGIC TO GIRLS, SCHOOL, AND OTHER SCARY THINGS

BY Lenore LOOK PICTURES BY LeUyen Pham

SCHOLASTIC INC.
New York Toronto London Auckland Sydney
Mexico City New Delhi Hong Kong Buenos Aires

ISBN-13: 978-0-545-19566-9
ISBN-10: 0-545-19566-7

Text copyright © 2008 by Lenore Look.
Illustrations copyright © 2008 by LeUyen Pham. All rights reserved.
Published by Scholastic Inc., 557 Broadway, New York, NY 10012, by arrangement with Schwartz & Wade Books, an imprint of Random House Children's Books, a division of Random House, Inc. SCHOLASTIC and associated logos are trademarks and/or registered trademarks of Scholastic Inc.

12 11 10 9 8 7 6 5 4 3 2 1   9 10 11 12 13 14/0

Printed in the U.S.A.   40

First Scholastic printing, October 2009

The text of this book is set in Adobe Caslon.
The illustrations are rendered in ink.
Book design by Rachael Cole

This book belongs to Sam Fisher, who inspired it.
—L.L.

To all the little Year of the Pigs born last year,
including two of my favorites: my nephew,
Dylan, and, of course, my own little Leo.
—L.P.

AUTHOR'S ACKNOWLEDGMENTS

"How vain it is to sit down to write when you have not
stood up to live."—Henry David Thoreau, journal entry,
19 August 1851

Those who have stood with me:
Madison Chen, whose reading is always invaluable.

Ann Kelley, who waited patiently for this book while
I procrastinated.

Vivian Low Fisher, who shared Sam with me.

Guillermo Francisco Nahoe, who threw the original, errant,
eponymous baseball.

Many thanks also to:
Jennifer Martin, Sam's teacher, for letting me come to class.

Dr. Elisa Shipon-Blum, for her insight into selective mutism.

The Concord Public Schools, for teaching Henry David
Thoreau in the second grade.

Johnny Look, for having a really strange goldfish.

CHAPTER ONE

Once Upon a Time

the first thing you should know about me is that my name is Alvin Ho.

I am afraid of many things.

Elevators.

Tunnels.

Bridges.

Airplanes.

Thunder.

Substitute teachers.

Kimchi.

Wasabi.

The dark.

Heights.

Scary movies.

Scary dreams.

Shots.

School.

If there were no school, my troubles would blast away, just like that. I would dig holes all day. I would play catch with my gunggung. I would watch cooking shows. I would keep an eye on things. It would be fantastic!

The second thing you should know about me is that even though I am afraid of many things, I am not afraid of anything that explodes. I love explosions. I was practically born with gunpowder in my blood! This is on account of I live in Concord, Massachusetts, which is hard to spell, but where there were explosions all over the place, when the American Revolutionary War started way before I was born.

The third thing you should know about me is

that I have a dog named Lucy and a brother named Calvin and a sister named Anibelly, who messes with my sticks and toys, eats my food, drinks my chocolate milk and gets in my way.

I am not as big as Calvin, but I am bigger than Anibelly, who isn't a baby anymore but doesn't go to school yet. I am sort of nearly almost medium . . . when I stand on tiptoe and stretch at the same time, I am finally almost visible in my class picture!

The fourth thing you should know about me is that I love Plastic Man, Wonder Woman, the Green Lantern, Concrete Man, Aquaman, King

Henry V and all the superheroes in the world. I know them from reading with my dad every night while my mom runs on the treadmill like a hamster on a wheel. My dad is a great reader for his age, which could be fifty or one hundred, it's hard to tell. He wears reading glasses and always puts one arm around me and his other arm around Anibelly and Calvin for support, on account of when you get to be that old, it is hard to do anything by yourself.

The fifth thing you should know about me is that once upon a time, before I went to school, I was a superhero. I was Firecracker Man! I ran around our house, full speed ahead, screaming at the top of my lungs while beating on a garbage can lid. I was as noisy as a firecracker on

Chinese New Year! My costume was great (my gunggung made it).

But now I am Firecracker Man only on weekends and holidays. There's just no time for it.

Being a superhero is hard work. You have to save the world. But going to school is even harder. You have to save yourself. Most days I can hardly even make it to the school bus. And when I arrive at school, I can't think. I can't read. I can't smile. I can't sing. I can't scream.

I can't even talk.

The sixth thing you should know about me is that I have never spoken a word in school. Even when I try with all my might, I always manage to say nothing at all. My voice works at home. It works in the car. It even works on the school bus. But as soon as I  get to school . . . I am as silent as a side of beef.

"You're like a piece of frozen sausage fallen off the truck," my brother, Calvin, likes to say. It is true. I am something like that.

No one really knows why I lose my voice at school, since I come from a long line of farmer-warriors who haven't had a scaredy bone in their bodies since 714 AD. In China my ancient grandpas and grandmas and aunts and uncles fought off leopards and tigers in their gardens the way Calvin and Anibelly and I fight off mosquitoes at Walden Pond. They weren't afraid of anything. I am afraid of everything.

CHAPTER TWO

Getting – Gulp – Ready for School

it was the last day of summer vacation and Calvin and I were in our room getting ready for the first day of school. He was going into the fourth grade and I was heading into second. Calvin was on the computer and I was sitting on my bed going over my PDK—Personal Disaster Kit.

When you're afraid of everything, it's very important to carry a PDK. It's like a PFD, a Personal Flotation Device, only heavier and with more parts. A PDK begins with the right box. It must not be too big, like a shoe box, or too small,

like a Band-Aid tin. A handle
on it is good, but a lock is
bad on account of it will
keep you out when you
need to get in. I use a
waterproof fly box
with compart-
ments, which is
just perfect.

You can put anything in a PDK, but mostly it
should be things that are useful in a disaster, such as:

A whistle. If I lose my voice, a whistle is very
handy.

A three-leaf clover (because I couldn't find a
four-leaf one).

Garlic. For fending off vampires and teachers.

Dental floss. Handy for trapping, wrapping,
tying and hanging things (out of Anibelly's
reach).

Band-Aids.

 A magnifying glass. For general curiosity, but can also be used to start a fire.

 A mirror. For sending signals, in case you can't start a fire.

 A bandana. For preventing smoke inhalation, in case you start the above fire, but can also be used as a sling or a tourniquet.

 A scary mask. For keeping girls away.

 Escape routes.

The problem with PDKs, as everyone knows, is that they need to be updated every year on account of you never know what you'll need in the next grade. Now that I could read and write without help, I was adding something I'd needed for a long time—emergency plans.

I read them aloud to Calvin:

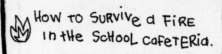

How to survive a fire in the school cafeteria.

1. Lie down. The freshest air is near the floor.

2. Crawl away from the flames.

3. Run.

And...

How to meet your new teacher →

1. Put on a scary mask.

2. Rub on garlic.

3. Stay back 100 feet.

And...

> **How to Survive SHOW-AND-TELL**
>
> 1. Show something spectacular.
> 2. Hold it high.
> 3. Turn it around.
> 4. Listen to the OOHS and AHHS.
>
>
>
> 5. Take a bow.

When I finished reading, I was very impressed with my plans.

But Calvin was not. "That's stupid," he said. Calvin is not supposed to use the s-word, it is bad.

"You can't say that," I said.

"Okay, it's *dumb*," said Calvin. "You're supposed to look your teacher in the eye, shake her hand and smile."

"But that's harder than putting on a scary mask," I said.

I am not too good at anything ever since I

started school, but Calvin is good at everything. He knows his multiplication tables, mostly. He has fantastic ideas for science projects. Most days he can finish his homework without falling asleep. And someday he will know something about everything because he is reading the entire encyclopedia online.

"Calvin," I said. "You're going to be the smartest person in the world."

"That's the whole idea," said Calvin, still reading. He needed to read pretty fast to give himself a jump-start on the fourth grade, which is when you have to speed-read to get yourself ready for middle school. He was up to the letter "D."

"Did you know that deer sleep only five minutes a day?" Calvin said.

"No," I said. "Calvin . . ."

Calvin ignored me and continued reading.

"The elephant is the only mammal that can't jump," he said.

Calvin was right. I've seen an elephant fly in a movie, but I've never seen one jump. "I need your help to finish my PDK," I said.

"I've already helped you," Calvin sighed. He did not look up.

"I need more help," I said. "I need emergency plans for making friends. None of the boys at school will play with me."

"That's because you're weird," said Calvin.

"I'm not weird," I said. "I have so-so performance anxiety disorder." It is true. I see a therapist for it.

"That's weird," said Calvin. He skipped ahead to "S."

"*You're* weird," I said.

"Did you know that the author William Shakespeare invented more than seventeen hundred words, including 'assassination' and 'bump'?"

I shook my head.

" 'Stewardesses' is the longest word you can type with only the left hand," said Calvin.

I growled.

Calvin stopped. "Okay," he said. "The first step in making friends is, don't talk so much. You need to be quiet. That is the first rule of being a good friend."

"Oh." I blinked. "But I can't talk in school!" I cried. "That's the problem!"

Calvin glared at me. "Maybe if you didn't use up all your words at home, you'd have some to use at school," he said.

I glared back.

"Okay," he said. "If I tell you, will you stop bothering me?"

"Okay," I agreed.

"Ready?" asked Calvin. "You better write fast."

So I did.

I read it twice.

Then I read it again.

CALViN'S RULES FOR
MAKING FRIENDS

1. Say HELLO.

2. JUST say hello.

3. TRADE baseball
   cards.

4. Trade MORE BASEBALL
   CARDS.

5. JUST TRade Baseball
   CARDS.

It wasn't perfect, but I put it into my PDK
and stopped bothering Calvin.

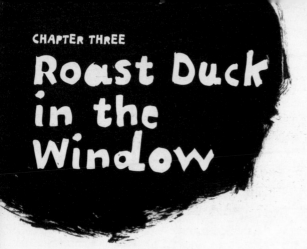

CHAPTER THREE

Roast Duck in the Window

after a while, I just had to bother Calvin again. He had stopped reading the encyclopedia online and was now sitting on the floor and holding a permanent marker in his hand.

"Whatcha doing?" I asked.

"I'm writing my name on everything I own," said Calvin. "That way, you'll have to ask for permission before you touch my stuff."

"Oh."

He wrote "Calvin Ho" on the

bottom of his sneakers. Then he wrote "C. Ho" in glistening black marker on the bottom of his baseball glove. "Calvin Ho" went inside his batting helmet. Finally, he began writing "Calvin Ho" inside his favorite books, which were also my favorite books.

It looked like I had better get started before everything belonged to Calvin!

So I grabbed another marker and wrote "Alvin Ho" on my baseball. It was not my play ball, but my special ball, kept in a clear plastic box on the shelf. Someone else had already written his name on it—Daisuke Matsuzaka, whose nickname is Dice-K. I can roll as fast as dice too, especially when I am Firecracker Man, so my name sure looked fantastic right next to his.

"Now that ball's good for nothing but playin'," said Calvin.

It was great news to me. I had always wanted to throw it.

But even better, Calvin seemed like he was now in a talking mood. So I gave him the bad news. "Calvin's Rules for Making Friends isn't going to work for me," I said. "I can't do anything on the list on account of I can't even say hello. Got any other ideas?"

"Hmmm," said Calvin, his marker in midair. "Are the other boys in your class bigger than you?"

"Mostly," I said, "but Pinky is bigger than everyone."

"Sometimes it helps if a friend is the same size as you," said Calvin. "Then you don't have to say anything."

"How come?" I asked.

"Dunno," said Calvin. "That's just the way it works."

Then Calvin went over to the computer, typed and clicked. "Stretching Exercises for Accelerated Growth" flashed across the screen. "See Results in Five Minutes! Amazing Results FAST!" There were all sorts of diagrams and instructions on how to grow a few inches. It was perfect! He printed a few pages, and we hurried outside to the backyard with them.

Summer wasn't quite over, but fall was already showing off with pretty leaves. Butter-, cinnamon-, orange- and burnt-toast-colored, the leaves looked like fireworks exploding in the golden afternoon light. And Anibelly was singing under them.

"Lalalalalalalala," Anibelly sang. "Lalalalalala."

Anibelly was digging holes, one of our favorite things to do. Her holes were not as good as mine—they weren't even real holes, just dimples— but she sure loved digging them.

"Lalalalalalala," she sang like a little bird. The garden hose was in one hand and one of my carved sticks was in the other.

I ran over. I nearly almost gave her a thumping, but I didn't. I remembered just in the nick of time that I am a gentleman. My dad taught me and Calvin the rules of being gentlemen. Rule

No. 1: No hitting, especially girls, unfortunately. If I remember only one rule it should be this, my dad said, and if I forget it, I will not be a man but a mushroom. Being a man would be a lot easier if Anibelly didn't mess with my things, eat my food, drink my chocolate milk or get in my way.

"Anibelly," I said, breathless. "That stick's been carved and it's not for digging, it's only for robbery and mayhem."

"Yup," said Anibelly. She stopped. She looked at the stick. My dad had shown me how to use a knife to take off the bark so that it would be smooth. I had a rare collection of these sticks against the back fence.

"And it's good for digging," Anibelly said. "Try it."

So I did. And so did Calvin. He digs better than anybody. He is a regular backhoe. Someday, he could become the world's best hole digger.

Dirt flew.

Water gushed.

It was great!

When our yard had more holes than the prairie dog exhibit at the zoo, we stopped.

"Anibelly, you're right," Calvin declared. "These sticks are good for digging. They're smooth in the hand, not rough."

Anibelly beamed. Calvin always has a good word for her.

"Now Alvin and I have work to do," said Calvin.

"Work?" Anibelly looked puzzled.

Calvin made a stirrup with his hands and I stuck my foot into it and he pushed me up into our apple tree. I grabbed a branch and hung from it.

"What kind of work is that?" asked Anibelly.

"It's a stretching exercise," said Calvin, "to make him taller. Being bigger will help him make friends in school."

"Oh," said Anibelly. She tilted like a teapot to look at me. "You look like a duck hanging in a Chinatown window."

"C'mon, let's help him," said Calvin. He

reached up and pulled on one foot and Anibelly copied, pulling on the other.

"See Results in Five Minutes!" said Calvin. "Amazing Results FAST!"

It hurt my armpits just a little, not too much. I could feel myself stretching like a rubber chicken.

Suddenly Anibelly let go. "Let's bake cookies with Mom!" she shrieked, and began running toward the house.

"Great idea!" said Calvin, taking off after Anibelly.

"Hey, wait!" I cried. "I want to bake too!"

Anibelly looked back but didn't stop. She was getting better at doing two things at once, like giving orders and running. "You keep stretching, Alvin," she said as she ran. "We'll bring you some cookies when they come piping hot out of the oven, okay? That way you'll be half grown by the time we get back!"

"Great idea!" I squeaked. Anibelly isn't in school yet, but she says things that sound as though she's already been through the sixth grade or something.

But it wasn't such a great idea for long. I could feel my grip slipping.

I couldn't hang on forever. I couldn't even hang on much longer!

But I couldn't jump either. I am afraid of heights. I could break some bones if I fell. So I

swung my legs up and draped my knees over the branch like on the monkey bars at school. It was a close call.

But this was not the monkey bars.

I was now upside down and even farther from the ground.

And I was . . . stuck.

"Calvin!" I yelled. "Help me down!"

There was no answer for a long time. . . .

Then the scent of cookies wafted from the house.

"Hey!" I screamed. I heard milk glasses clinking, followed by the muffled voices of a TV cooking show.

Then the sound of Anibelly singing, "Lalalalalalalalalalala."

"Anibelly!" I screamed. "Help!"

"Lalalalalalalalalalala," sang Anibelly.

"Mom!" I squawked.

My breath puffed out in clouds. My face froze.

My nose ran. My
ears rang. My head spun.
Then . . . I had an itch
I couldn't reach.

But that wasn't
the worst of it.

It was getting
DARK. The wind
moved and the leaves

applauded. The garden hose hissed and slithered.
The grass disappeared, and in its place roared a
black, black sea.

"Aaaaaaaaaaaaaaaaaaaaaaaack!" I screamed.

Somewhere a piano played.

Video games blasted.

And Anibelly sang, "Lalalalalalalalalala."

I wanted to cry. So I did. I squeezed the
branch with my knees and cried full blast. Crying is really great, even upside down. Everything
is always better afterward.

And it was. Soon I heard Louise coughing up
the driveway. Louise is my dad's wasabi-green

car, which he loves more than fireworks. My dad was home! My dad is *da dad*, which means he's the best. He would save me, he always does.

"DAD!" I yelled. "DAAAAAD! HELP ME! DAAD! I'M IN THE TREEEEE!" I screamed as loudly as I could.

There was only one problem. No sound came out of my mouth. My voice was all in my head.

Out there in the cold . . . in the dark . . . in the grasp of the evil tree, perched above the hungry sea . . . I was too scared to speak . . . and school hadn't even begun!

•●•●•

"Oh, you poor thing," said my mom, rolling me up in a blanket before carrying me into the house. "How did we forget you?"

It is easy to forget me. I don't make much noise whenever I am scared out of my wits. And like my dad says, "Out of sight, out of mind," which means if you don't see me, you won't think of me either.

But finally, when my mom saw my empty place at the dinner table, she thought of me.

My mom is *da mom*. She never had another life, like my dad, who was probably secretly a gung fu action hero spymaster assassin before he was a dad. She was always a mom—she was practically born that way—but that's okay. She is really super-duper. She is not afraid of heights. She can climb a tree in two seconds flat and tear me—poor thing—from the grasp of the evil tree, just like that.

I love it when she calls me that: poor thing. It was almost worth hanging like a roast duck to hear it. Poor thing.

CHAPTER FOUR

Allergic to School

"**when i was** your age . . . ," my dad said at breakfast the next day, "I was scared of school too. Worse, I was never a superhero before I went to school, so it was very rough."

My dad is not superhero material, but he has read practically everything ever written about superheroes and so knows us from beginning to end, which explains a lot about him.

"Just hold your head high," said my dad, "and be a gentleman."

"But I feel sick," I said.

My dad put a hand on my forehead.

"No fever," he said.

"Are you sure?" I looked at his hands. They are thick like baseball mitts. It was a wonder he could feel anything through them.

"Where does it hurt?" he asked.

"All over," I said. It was true; I was not making it up. I must have grown at least two inches from stretching so long in the tree. And growing hurts, as everyone knows.

I gave a little moan.

"Hmmm," said my dad.

I moaned a little more.

"You are not sick," said my dad.

"But I will be," I said. "I will be very, very sick. I'm allergic to school, *severely* allergic."

My dad looked at me.

"Alvin," he said firmly, putting one of his mitts on my shoulder.

"Yes, Dad."

"You will be okay, son," he said. I love it when he calls me that. Son.

I felt a little better. Maybe my dad was right, maybe I would be okay. A good word from my dad changes everything. Besides, if I missed the bus, my dad might have a few other words for me. So I dashed out of the house and caught up with Calvin just as the bus was pulling up to the end of our driveway.

"Bye, Alvin!" cried Anibelly. "Bye, Calvin!"

"Bye, Anibelly!" We waved and climbed on.

The wheels on the bus went round and round.

I was okay.

I clutched my PDK and sat next to Calvin in the back of the bus where all the fourth graders sit. The big kids screamed their heads off. I screamed my head off. We bounced up and down.

"You will be okay, son," my dad's voice echoed between my ears.

I smiled at Calvin. And Calvin smiled back.

I was okay.

Then we arrived at school.

My sneakers landed like a couple of cement blocks when I got off the bus. *Pfuump, pfuump.*

My stomach turned like a washing machine when I got inside.

I found the door that said "Second Grade, Miss Pestalozzi."

My throat tightened.

"Welcome," said a lady. "I'm Miss P."

I stopped dead in my tracks. Her hair was shiny and her skin was clean. She smelled like fresh laundry out of the dryer. She smiled at me.

But I did not smile back. I hardly even looked at her. I clutched my PDK.

I felt dizzy.

I looked around. The room was bright and neat. The walls were blank except for a picture of Henry David Thoreau and another picture of a small cabin. It is a copycat version of the original cabin that Henry had built at Walden Pond with his own hands.

"Henry David Thoreau is my hero," Esha said to her friend Flea. "You know, he kept a really cool journal. My sister says we get to read parts of it in second grade."

Everyone pushed past me. Eli shoved Scooter and Scooter shoved back. "You're it!" cried Scooter, tagging Eli, who tripped backward over Jules, who was curled on the floor waiting for Sam to leapfrog. Then Hobson and Nhia scuttled across the room like two crabs in a death lock. They were terrific!

Everything whirled around me. I was in the middle of it, but I was not in it at all.

So far, second grade wasn't any different from

first grade, which wasn't any different from kindergarten.

I was thinking about running and hiding, when . . .

"Wanna be desk buddies again?" It was Flea. She was my desk buddy in first grade. She is a girl.

I wanted to say no way. Nobody wants a girl desk buddy, except for maybe a girl. The scary thing about girls is that they are not boys. Most girls are no good at robbery and mayhem. They can't punch. But they can kick, which hurts. They skip rope too fast. They are boring. I opened my mouth to tell her all this, but . . .

My tongue turned into sandpaper.

Nothing came out.

"C'mon," said Flea, pulling out the chair next to her. "You can sit with me and Esha."

Everyone was choosing their seat and sitting down. Soon it would be too late to sit with the boys.

I opened my mouth. I wished for my voice. I wished and wished and wished. But nothing came out.

Finally, I slumped into the chair.

I was not okay.

I was so allergic to school, but I was even more allergic to girls.

CHAPTER FIVE

The Trouble with the S-Word

not being able to talk in school is a terrible problem. But having a girl desk buddy is even worse; it is the kiss of death.

At recess, I heard:

Alvin and Flea sitting in a tree.
K-I-S-S-I-N-G
First comes love.
Then comes marriage.
Then comes Alvin with a baby carriage!

Oooh. It really fried my rice.

But the real problem with having a girl desk buddy is that she will follow you home no matter how hard you try to ditch her. And it is hard to ditch her when the bus stops at the end of your driveway and nearly everyone gets off and your house is right there and the whole gang can see that a girl is going up your driveway.

"Hi, Mrs. Ho!" called Flea as soon as we reached the top.

"Hello, Sophie," said my mom, smiling and using Flea's real name. "It's very nice to see you."

Mouths dropped open at the bottom of the driveway. Pinky, Jules, Sam, Nhia, Eli, Scooter and Hobson, the whole gang, stood speechless.

"It's nice to see you too," said Flea, blinking her one good eye at my mom. If there is anything good about Flea, it is this: she wears an eye patch over one eye, like a pirate. Also one of her legs is longer than the other, like a peg leg, which is also marvelous. "I'm Alvin's desk buddy again this year."

"That's wonderful," said my mom, smiling even more and holding the door open. "Alvin is very lucky."

"Yup," said Flea. "He's very lucky."

"Would you like to come in for afternoon tea and rice crackers?"

I narrowed my eyes at Flea, which meant she had better say no and go away.

And my mom narrowed her eyes at me, which meant I had better behave like a gentleman or I had something coming.

"I'd love to!" said Flea, and she stepped right inside my house and then sat right down at my place in the kitchen across from Anibelly.

Worse, Lucy came and gave her the kiss that she usually gives to me.

"It's a terrible problem not being able to talk at school," Flea said right off. "So having the right desk buddy makes a real difference."

My mom nodded. She had that look on her face that said she thought Flea was a darling girl.

"It's a big responsibility," said Flea. "So I'm even more prepared this year than last year."

"You have a PDK?" asked Anibelly.

"No," said Flea. "But I made this." She reached into her backpack and pulled out a book. *The Book on Alvin*, it said on the cover. "I wrote the book on Alvin," said Flea.

Then Flea proudly opened her book.

Page one: "'Alvin can talk with his eyes,'" Flea read loud and clear.

Page two: there was a drawing of two eyes, my two eyes. "'These eyes mean he's thinking,'" I read.

Flea nodded. She turned the page.

Page three: there was a drawing of two more of my eyes. "'These eyes mean he's okay,'" read Flea.

Page four: a pair of anxious eyes. "These eyes mean he has to go pee!" exclaimed Anibelly without reading.

"Hey!" I said.

Page five: a pair of big round eyes. "'And these eyes mean he has bingo!'" read Flea.

"What a great book!" said my mom with that smile on her face that said she thought Flea was a very clever girl, and I had still better be a gentleman or else! "You are very observant," my mom added.

Flea beamed. "Thank you," she said. "People

think Alvin's uncommunicative, but he's really not."

"Alvin should be proud to have a friend like you," said my mom. She was so pleased that she brought out a special treat, two-thousand-year-old dragon's beard candy in a box, and offered it to Flea first.

As if that weren't enough, Flea asked for chopsticks.

Then she *sluuurp*ed her tea like she really meant it and pinched a dragon's beard candy between her chopsticks and popped it right into her mouth. She even chewed with her mouth closed the *whole* time.

"I saw dragon's beard candy on a cooking show once," said Flea, dabbing her lips with a napkin. "It's made of eight thousand strands of sugar wrapped around nuts and coconut and sesame seeds."

My mom beamed.

"I'm taking Aggression for Girls," Flea went on. "It's a combination of kickboxing and karate and it's supposed to make me stronger . . . and I

got a goldfish this summer. His name is
Boatswain. He watches action movies
and swims around only during
commercials." She smiled and reached
for another piece of dragon's beard.

I could hardly stand it.

"I think it's a stupid book," I blurted.
"And you're a stupid girl."

Flea gasped. She clasped *The Book on
Alvin* to her chest. Her mouth fell open,
and some beard strands fell out.

"Alvin Ho!" said my mom. "You
apologize right now!"

I hung my head. I had used the
s-word.

I crossed my chopsticks this way.

Then I crossed my chopsticks that way.

My mom was giving me *that* look, which
meant that I had better apologize or she would
make dragon's beard out of me.

Yoctoseconds turned into zeptoseconds, turned
into attoseconds, turned into a blink of an eye,

then into a heartbeat. Then my life crawled before my eyes.

"Sorry," I finally peeped.

Tears filled Flea's eye.

It was not a good sign. I had a terrible feeling that a gentleman would never make a girl cry, even a girl with only one eye.

Flea slipped *The Book on Alvin* into her backpack and, without a word, headed out the door.

I was so relieved and happy to see her go, I felt like dancing! If I had danced, the new look on my mom's face said, she would have broken my legs.

So I dashed out after Flea. I had a feeling that it was the gentleman thing to do, but I didn't really know, I couldn't remember.

"Hey . . . ," I huffed when I caught up with her. But Flea did not stop. She moves rather fast for someone who can see only half of everything and walks on uneven legs.

"Stop!" I said.

Flea stopped. She blinked her eye. She crossed her arms.

I breathed in. And I breathed out. I did not feel so good. I was on the sidewalk, in broad daylight—gulp—with a girl.

"Okay," I said.

"Okay, what?" said Flea.

"Okay, I'm going to mean it this time," I said.

Flea waited.

I waited.

A car rolled by.

I leaned over to see what was in the gutter.

Nothing.

Then I looked up to see if there might be any giant meteorites heading for Flea.

None.

So finally, I blurted, "I'm sorry that it's a weird book and that you're a weird girl."

POW!

I think it was an uppercut. I'd seen it on Saturday-afternoon boxing with my pohpoh. An uppercut is when you curl your arm like you're picking up a pail of rocks and you send your fist into your opponent's jaw from the bottom up. I lifted off my feet and landed on my butt. "*Owwwwwww!*" I felt like crying. So I did.

Just as I was about to duke it back to Flea, a police car rolled by. And everyone knows that a police car is much more interesting than punching a girl. It was a good thing that the police car rolled by because I come from a long line of farmer-warriors in China who have been duking it out since 714 AD and it looked like Flea had taken lessons or something and knew what she was doing, so we would have battled to the death for sure. And it is hard to say how scary that would have been.

CHAPTER SIX

Minutemen vs. Redcoats

if flea were a boy, everything would be different. First, she wouldn't have ignored me all morning. Second, things would have improved between us on account of boys have more respect for one another after a good pounding. But Flea is not a boy. She is a girl. And girls are weird even if they wear a cool eye patch, drag a cool peg leg and know how to throw a mean uppercut.

I was thinking about all this when . . .

"Alvin?" a voice called. "Alvin?"

My heart stopped. It was Miss P. She is very nice, but she has a habit of calling on you when you least expect it. Everyone was looking at me over the tops of their books and holding their breath. . . .

The hand on the clock clicked *tick, tick, tick.*

Someone's toe tapped *toc, toc, toc.*

My heart thumped *boom, boom, boom.*

I couldn't breathe in. I couldn't breathe out.

"Alvin," said Miss P. "Would you like to skip your turn?"

It was reading class. We were reading something about Henry David Thoreau's furniture. He had only three chairs: one for being by himself, two for a friend, and three for a party. Normally, I like reading. Like my dad, I am a great reader for my age. I can make my voice go up and down and pause at all the commas and periods, just like my dad, to make everything super-duper exciting. But in school . . .

Henry David Thoreau

I opened my mouth. The words on the page were supposed to roll right off my tongue . . . but nothing did.

I was *not* skipping my turn, but it always *looks* like I am.

If there is anything good about reading class it is this: history class comes next.

History class is not like reading class. History is all about the American Revolutionary War, which happened back when everyone was having fights and firing cannons left and right and enjoying all sorts of explosions without getting busted.

If you live in Concord, Massachusetts, which is hard to spell, it is hard not to like history. My gunggung says it has something to do with feng shui, which is the Chinese way of saying some places are more exciting than others. The only problem with Concord is that there are no volcanoes. If there were a volcano with explosions now and then, it would be the most exciting place in the world!

The best thing about history, as everyone knows, is that you can play it at recess.

Our favorite game is Patriots' Day, which is based on the most exciting day of the year, April 19, which is the day when the American Revolutionary War began back in 1775. Every year on that day the church bells ring like crazy, just like they rang long ago, to call the Minutemen out from their homes to fight the Redcoats. The Minutemen were the good guys. They were ready to march or fight at a minute's notice. And the Redcoats were the bad guys, sent by the King of England to capture the gunpowder and explosives that the Minutemen had hidden all over Concord.

This is how to play Patriots' Day.

First, the Redcoats march in across the playground from their hiding place behind the cafeteria.

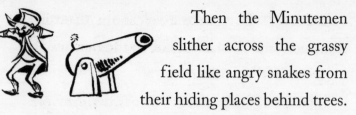

Then the Minutemen slither across the grassy field like angry snakes from their hiding places behind trees. They meet at the Old North Bridge, which is really the monkey bars, where the Redcoats won't let the Minutemen swing across. The Minutemen begin to swing anyway because the monkey bars belong to them, and the British say no way, they've just captured the monkey bars, so they shoot the Minutemen, who then drop dead on the wood chips.

Then the British Redcoats want to pretend to be dead too, but the Minutemen won't let them. The Redcoats pretend to be dead anyway, but the Minutemen won't stand for it so they duke it out, just like they did back in historic times. It is mayhem and chaos! It is the beginning of the American Revolution!

But before you can have a revolution, you have to choose sides.

"You guys on this side are the Minutemen,"

said Pinky, who usually does all the choosing.
"And you guys on that side are the Redcoats." He
pointed to everyone but me.

I wanted to play too, so I said with my eyes

that I wanted to be a Minuteman or a Redcoat, it didn't matter to me, war was war.

"Hey, how about Alvin?" asked Sam. He doesn't like leaving anyone out.

I stood up as tall as I could.

"Alvin who?" asked Pinky. He looked around. He looked up and down. Then he looked right through me. "Who's Alvin?"

Pinky is no pinky. He has been the biggest boy in my class since kindergarten because he started school late. And he's also the leader of the gang, which means if he doesn't play with me, the other boys won't either.

I wished with all my might that Pinky would let me play. But he never does. Then I wished with all my might that I could just scream! But I couldn't. I could only stamp my foot, which didn't help. I was buzzing mad like my dad's electric razor, but I couldn't buzz!

"The British are coming! The British are coming!" Pinky yelled to start the game. He was

pretending to be Samuel Prescott, the local hero who warned Concord that the enemy was approaching. It is not fair that Pinky is always Samuel Prescott, but he is the biggest boy. And the biggest boy can be whoever he wants.

"God save the king!" yelled Jules. Jules was the leader of the Redcoats.

"God save the Minutemen!" screamed Sam.

"Charge!" everyone yelled.

The gang headed for the monkey bars, where the Minutemen pounded the Redcoats and the Redcoats thumped the Minutemen until the playground monitor came and called a time-out. It was fantastic!

Even though I wasn't a Minuteman or a Redcoat, I played dead at the end anyway because there's no law stopping anyone from lying on the soft wood chips and closing their eyes.

You can't live in Concord without loving history, but I sure wished that I loved recess too.

CHAPTER SEVEN

The Best Way to Avoid School

the best way to avoid school, as everyone knows, is to get sick.

But not all sicknesses are created equal. Some are better than others.

Tonsillitis, for example, is pretty good. You get all the Italian ice you want. It is my dream to have tonsillitis someday.

Appendicitis is good too, but not as good as a *burst* appendix, which gets you a ride in a wailing ambulance speeding through all the red lights on Route 62 to Emerson Hospital. This happened when Calvin's appendix burst and our mom found him on the kitchen floor. He has all the luck!

The flu is okay, but it's not great. You only get ginger ale and crackers, which is a real rip-off, but usually you get to watch all the cooking shows and cartoons you want.

The common cold? One bad-tasting zinc drop, some tissues and you're back in school the next day.

Medical mysteries? If you get foreign-accent syndrome or barking madness or squeaky chalk phobia, forget it. You're back in school the *same* day.

So you have to be patient. It's like choosing a car, or a house; my mom says you shouldn't jump at the first offer because a better deal might be right around the corner.

And it was.

One day, Jules was out—with chicken pox.

"Don't go near Jules's house," Miss P warned our class. "It'll take two weeks for all the blisters to scab over completely. Until then, Jules is highly contagious."

Highly contagious?

I felt like dancing!

I nearly burst like fireworks!

But I didn't.

I had to wait until after school.

·•·•·

It was hard *not* to go near Jules's house. It is on the way to everything. It is as though Jules's house is a big magnet and I am an iron filing, and every time I so much as step out of my house, I am yanked toward it, just like that.

When I finished after-school tea with my mom and finally stepped out of my house, that was exactly what happened! I was sucked by such a powerful force toward Jules's house that I could barely even pick up the fat frog in the gutter on my way. And when I got to Jules's house, there was already a line behind the tall bushes in front, just like the line at the cinema when there's a scary movie playing.

"Hey, guys," I said.

"Shhhhhhhh," hissed Eli. "Stay low or Jules's mom will see us and we'll all get sent home."

"Wait your turn or shove off," said Hobson, who always gives you a choice. "This is a top-secret under-cover operation. We go in one at a time, or we don't go in at all."

"Okay," I said. "I'll wait."

"*Urrrrrgh*," said the frog in my hands.

"What's that you got? A frog?" asked Nhia.

"Yup," I said.

I set the frog in the grass and everyone leaped around trying to catch it for a while. It was fabulous! Then before I knew it, it was my turn. I caught my frog, rushed around the side of the house and ran right into Pinky under Jules's window.

"Watch where you're going," said Pinky. He held out a can. On the can was a label:

> *One-minute visit: 50¢*
> *Jump into bed: $1*

"You got a dollar?" Pinky asked.

I gasped. Normally, Pinky does not speak to me. Usually I do not show up on his radar, not one bleep, not even a flicker.

But I was flickering now!

I shook my head. I did not have a dollar.

"You got fifty cents?"

"No."

"I'll take that frog, then," said Pinky.

"No way," I said, tucking the frog into my armpit. "It's for Jules."

"No dollar, no frog, no service," said Pinky.

"Wait," I said, remembering an unchewed piece of gum in my back pocket. I took it out. It was warm and soft.

Pinky grabbed the gum, unwrapped it and stuffed it into his cheek. "Okay," he said, gnawing. "You get a minute."

I took my frog and hopped through Jules's window.

Jules was in bed.

I gave my frog to Jules.

"Thanks," said Jules.

"Urggggh-rrrrgh," said the frog. "Urrrrggggh."

"So where's the chicken?" I asked, glancing around Jules's room.

"I was wondering that myself," said Jules. "I wish I knew."

I was really disappointed. How do you catch chicken pox without first catching a chicken?

"I came to catch the *chicken* pox," I said. "Not
the plain pox."

But the plain pox wasn't too shabby. It had
turned Jules's head into a potato covered with red
eyes. Some eyes were crying, others were crusty
like sugar on a cookie. It was great! Jules had
never looked scarier!

"So whatcha doin'?" I asked.

"Nothing," said Jules. "Well, maybe I'm scratching a little."

Jules was scratching like crazy. I do not know if Jules is a girl or a boy. Sometimes Jules plays with the boys, and other times Jules plays with the girls. "Jules" could stand for "Julian" or it could stand for "Julia."  It is hard to tell. The blisters didn't help either. In fact, they made Jules look like neither boy nor girl. Instead, Jules looked a good deal like an alien. A real live alien potato fresh off a UFO.

"You're so lucky!" I said. "I'd love to look like that."

"Yeah," said Jules. "It's really great except for the itching."

"You got any you can't reach?" I asked.

"Yeah, right up the middle of my back," said Jules, squirming.

So I gave Jules a hand. I think it is one of the

rules of being a gentleman, but I don't really know, I can't remember.

"Thanks," said Jules.

"Anytime," I said.

"Time's up!" Pinky hissed from the window.

"Dude," I said.

"Dude," said Jules.

•••••

None of us caught a chicken or even saw one. So none of us broke out with the chicken pox that day. Or the plain pox either. It was a terrible disappointment.

Then a long time later . . . just when we'd forgotten all about Jules and the chicken pox, and none of us were trying to catch anything anymore . . . a miracle happened.

Our art teacher, Mr. Gruenert, was showing us famous self-portraits one warm afternoon.

Frida Kahlo looked a little itchy to me with branches coming out of her hair.

Paul Gauguin looked a bit feverish because he was in Tahiti, where it's really hot.

And Vincent van Gogh, in his scratchy straw hat, *definitely* looked itchy.

Very itchy.

Then we got mirrors and brushes so that we could paint our own self-portraits. My self-portrait was going to be a masterpiece, but strangely . . . I didn't feel like painting. I didn't feel like doing anything at all.

"You boys look a little strange," said Mr. Gruenert.

I felt strange.

Then I looked into the mirror. Something scary stared back.

"Aaaaaaaaaaaaaaaaaaaaaaaaaack!" screamed the whole gang. They were looking in their mirrors too!

Then Flea, who was next to me, looked at me. *"Aaaaaaaaaaaaieeeeeeeeeee!"* she shrieked, spilling her paints.

The other girls screamed too. Some ran fast. Others ran faster.

You'd think we were a bunch of aliens or something.

School shut down for two weeks and a half after that. There was a story about us in the newspaper so that people as far away as Andover, Massachusetts, which is also hard to spell, read about the great chicken pox epidemic in Concord. We were famous! The newspaper said . . .

The first victim had been carefully quarantined.

All the children had been warned to keep away.

How the epidemic ever got started was a complete mystery.

CHAPTER EIGHT

Johnny Astro

having school shut down was really fabulous.

Even if it meant scratching like crazy.

I wore my Firecracker Man outfit all day.

I didn't have to carry my PDK.

I didn't have to worry about being a gentleman.

Best of all, I didn't have to sit next to a girl, except for Anibelly, who doesn't count on account of she's my sister and there's just no avoiding that.

Somehow Calvin and Anibelly also got the chicken pox and together we watched all the cooking shows we wanted.

Our mom made us Italian ices.

Our pohpoh rubbed us with lotion.

Our gunggung told us stories about when he was little and had the chicken pox in China. His family had chickens. He chased the chickens. The chickens chased him. Then he got the pox. He was so lucky!

We chilled out completely.

Even my dad stayed home a couple of days to chill so that my mom could go to work. And whenever he chills, he reaches for his favorite toy—Johnny Astro.

It is a special occasion whenever my dad plays with his Johnny Astro. It means he is in a really good mood. And playing with the toy puts him in an out-of-this-galaxy mood. Best of all, it means that I get my dad all to myself. Calvin and Anibelly always sneak away whenever Johnny Astro comes out. We've watched Johnny Astro all our lives, and now neither one of them enjoys watching it anymore. But I do.

"When I was your age . . . ," my dad began. He always begins with a story about being my age whenever he reaches for his Johnny Astro. "There was nothing I loved more than Johnny Astro. Not my ant farm, not my walkie-talkie, not my power drill, not even . . . my baseball card collection."

I love stories about when my dad was a kid. Sometimes they are funny, like how it used to snow so much they had to dig tunnels through the snow for air, and sometimes they aren't funny, like when his yehyeh died and everyone was so sad they forgot to feed YehYeh's bird, so his bird died too.

"When I was your age," my dad continued, "Johnny Astro made me very popular. Everyone wanted to play with me because I had a Johnny Astro."

"Everyone?"

"Absolutely," said my dad. "No one ever saw a toy like this. No one."

I read the box. "Johnny Astro," it said. "Really Flies. No Wires. No Connections. FLY YOUR SPACE CRAFT ANYWHERE."

"If you can fly one of these," my dad said breathlessly, "you can fly anything."

He put batteries into the plastic control panel and flipped the switch. A fan whirred softly and he moved the stick shift like a pilot.

Suddenly a balloon with an astronaut launched into the air! The balloon swirled and hovered silently above our heads as if by magic.

I blinked rapidly. I breathed rapidly. Fireworks burst inside my eyes.

"You can take off . . . you can land it . . . fire the propulsion, knock it down, capture it, fly it again," said my dad. "To the moon—at full throttle!"

The balloon went up, up, up, and landed on a high shelf. Then it floated off the shelf as if lifted by an invisible hand.

"Can I try?" I asked. I had watched my dad play a million times, but I had never played with it, not even once. But I had the pox . . . and who could say no to a poor thing with pox?

"Only . . . if you're careful," said my dad. "It takes a special touch."

"Cross my heart," I said.

I commandeered Johnny Astro up and over our heads and then smoothly onto a landing pad on the coffee table.

My dad was very impressed. "Amazing!" he said, blinking rapidly. "You're as astonishing as I was at your age! You're top gun."

He shook his head.

He wiped his eyes.

He put his hand on my back.

"Someday," my dad said in a low whisper, "this will be yours."

I gasped. I didn't know what to say. My dad had *never* said that before. And my dad *always* means what he says. I think it is one of the rules of being a gentleman, but I don't really know, I can't remember.

I only wished that Calvin and Anibelly had

been there to hear it too, in case my ears were playing tricks on me, which they sometimes do.

"M-m-mine?" I could hardly say it.

My dad nodded. "Sure, son," he said.

•●•●•

That night I had a dream that I was Johnny Astro himself! I got into Johnny Astro's balloon and blasted straight into orbit. I went over the tops of everything, even the moon! I sailed across the inky sky. It was thrilling! Everything was great . . .

Until I looked down.

Then nothing was great. I felt dizzy. Our driveway pinwheeled under my sneakers.

Then I crash-landed and woke up.

I ran downstairs.

I looked up.

And there, in the moonlight, on the top shelf of the highest bookcase, was Johnny Astro, safe and sound.

TGID. Thank God it was only a dream.

CHAPTER NINE

A Real Nightmare

my dad is really good at taking care of his things. Maybe it is one of the rules of being a gentleman, but I don't really know, I can't remember. "Take care of your things," my dad likes to say, "and your things will take care of you."

He takes such good care of his car, Louise, for example, that she will probably run for a third geological age, although

she already has one transmission in the junkyard, which, my mom says, is the car equivalent of having one foot in the grave.

My dad also takes good care of our house and our yard. He can use a hammer. He can climb a ladder. He can climb down too, usually. And he owns a power drill in a box.

He takes really good care of his children too. Just look at us—a couple of weeks of scratching ourselves to death and we were practically normal again, on our way back to school.

So when my dad wasn't playing with his Johnny Astro, he kept it in its box and set the box on the top shelf of the highest bookcase for safekeeping.

The Johnny Astro sure was amazing, even sitting in its box. I headed into the living room to look at it one last time before going to school. "Johnny Astro made me very popular," my dad's voice replayed itself in my ears. "Everyone wanted to play with me. . . ."

"Johnny Astro," I read across the box for the

millionth time. "Really Flies. No Wires. No Connections. FLY YOUR SPACE CRAFT ANYWHERE."

I stared, unblinking.

I shifted my PDK under my arm.

I swallowed.

"Alvin," my mom yelled from the kitchen. "Hurry, honey, your bus is almost here!"

"Coming, Mom!" I yelled back.

But first . . . all I needed was a stool and to str—eeeee—eeetch until I could reach it. Johnny Astro was perfect for show-and-tell.

"Someday," my dad's low whisper filled my ears, "this will be yours."

Someday. I had no idea that someday would be today!

"Thanks, Dad," I whispered. "You're the best." I even remembered my manners.

Then I slid the box into a large shopping bag . . . and I slipped out the door.

"What's that?" Pinky asked as soon as I got on the bus.

I gasped. I could hardly believe it. I was already flickering on Pinky's radar!

"Johnny Astro," I said.

"What's Johnny Astro?"

"The greatest toy ever made," I said.

"Never heard of it," said Pinky. "What does it do?"

"I'll show you at show-and-tell," I said.

"But you don't do show-and-tell," said Hobson.

"I do too," I protested.

"You show, but you never tell," said Sam.

Sam was right, I never tell. But I was fabulous at show. I knew how to pick 'em. If something tells a story, and as long as I can reach it and it is something I can carry without using a wheelbarrow, it is probably perfect. I've brought in all sorts of treasures . . . my dad's fantastic reading glasses . . . my mom's pearl necklace that she looks so good in . . . Calvin's baseball card collection.

And now Johnny Astro.

"If this is the greatest toy ever made, you should show-and-tell *now*," said Pinky, "*before* we get to school, or we'll never know what you wanted to say."

It made perfect sense. I could hardly wait anyway. I pulled the box out of the bag.

The gang read the box.

All jaws dropped open.

All tongues fell out.

"That's just the box," I said. "Wait till you see it in action!" I fingered the edge of the cover.

"Open it," Sam pleaded. "Open it."

I held my breath.

I wanted to open it. I wanted to show the gang the most fabulous toy ever made. I couldn't wait.

Whoosh. I lifted the cover. An old smell of fun and excitement filled our noses.

Then *whoosh*. The bus rounded a corner.

And we rounded in our seats.

And when we all sat back up . . . Johnny Astro
didn't look the same. There were a few pieces . . .
missing.

They were not in the box.

They were not in the bag.

Or in the aisle.

Or under the seats.

They were *nowhere* to be seen.

I was not even sure which pieces were missing. But there were a few empty spaces in the plastic package where there should have been parts.

"OH NO!" I cried. "MY DAD'S GOING TO KILL ME!"

The noise on the bus went round and round. It was so loud that my voice got lost. No one turned around. Even the driver's eyes, which usually lift into her mirror whenever there is an extraordinary outburst, did not shift.

I swallowed. I blinked. I did my best not to cry. The wheels on the bus went round and round. I bounced up and down. But then a tear rolled down my cheek. Then another. And another. Before I knew it, I was crying full blast. Crying is really great. Everything is better afterward . . .

Except when the next stop is school.

And when you walk into class, you find a substitute teacher.

"Alvin Ho," called the sub. She was taking attendance, which is where most of my troubles usually begin with subs.

I opened my PDK. I needed an escape route.

"Alvin," the sub called again.

"Here," answered Flea.

"You are Alvin Ho?" asked the sub.

"No, ma'am, I'm Flea," said Flea. "That's Alvin." She pointed at me.

The sub looked at Flea and then at me, over the top of her glasses. "He can answer for himself," she said.

"No he can't," said Flea.

"Why not?"

"He just can't," said Flea. "He's Alvin Ho."

The sub's eyebrows arched like two unconnected bridges. "I will have no funny business in my classroom today, is that clear?" said the sub.

Flea nodded. Then her lips curled in, which meant that she had more to say. "Alvin talks normally at home," Flea continued, "but at school he only talks with his eyes."

"Oh?"

"Just watch his eyes," said Flea.

I rolled my eyes, not on purpose, they just rolled on their own like a couple of loose pearls from my mom's necklace the time I borrowed it for show-and-tell.

"Oops," said Flea.

"Is this a joke?" asked the sub.

"No, ma'am." Flea shook her head.

The sub looked puzzled. "No one mentioned a special-needs student. . . ."

"Alvin's not special," Flea explained matter-of-factly. "He just doesn't speak in school."

The sub fixed her gaze on Flea. Then she locked her gaze on me. It meant that I needed to be on my best behavior.

Fortunately, I've had lots of practice in good behavior. I knew what to do. I kept my eyes low. I kept my hands in plain sight. I stayed in my seat.

Then show-and-tell began.

Jules showed a pox scab.

"Ah, that's nothing," said Eli. So then Eli showed his. It was redder than Jules's.

But it wasn't redder than Hobson's, which was *crimson*.

But that was nothing compared to Esha's, which was practically still oozing.

Then everyone began raising their shirts and lowering their pants to see who had the biggest and ugliest scab of all. It was fabulous!

Then the substitute said that that was enough of the scabs. But some of us had taken off so much of our clothing by then that it took a while to get it all back on.

Then the dreaded moment came.

"Alvin," said the sub. "Do you have a show-and-tell?"

I froze. I avoided eye contact.

I held my breath. I sucked in my gut. I clutched my PDK.

"His show-and-tell met with some misfortune on the bus this morning," said Flea helpfully. "So it can't be shown."

"Misfortune?" said the sub. She gave me the

stare that said I wasn't yet finished with misfortune.

So, slowly, I pulled out the box.

"Johnny Astro!" gasped the sub. "I had one of these. It's the best toy in the world! It really flies! You can fire it up, send it into orbit and bring it down again. It is absolutely spectacular!"

The class went silent. No one moved. No one even breathed.

The sub got very quiet. She wiped her eyes. "Nothing else like it was ever made," she sighed.

Then she smiled at me.

And I smiled back just a little. Maybe it is even a gentleman's rule to smile back when a lady smiles at you, but I don't really know, I can't remember.

For a sub, I guess she was okay.

As for show-and-tell, it was the best thing I had ever brought in. Everyone wanted to play with me at recess.

"We'll get it up in the air in no time," said

Pinky, carrying the box out to the playground. "I'll hold it while you fix it."

I nodded.

Then we lifted off the cover. The missing pieces were back! But they were wrecked.

"I found them in the back of the bus," said Flea. "And put them back in there for you."

"Don't worry," said Eli, whose father fixes cars. "I can fix anything. My dad showed me how."

"I can do origami," said Sam. "I'll make you a new balloon!"

"Here are some Band-Aids," said Eli, peeling a dirty one from each elbow.

"And I've got spray paint at home if you want to come over after school," said Nhia.

I opened my PDK. There were instructions for surviving practically every disaster except a Johnny Astro disastro. That's the problem with PDKs, you never know what you're missing until you are missing it.

"Alvin," said Flea, putting a hand on my shoulder. "People will think you were careless, but you really weren't."

"It was an accident," said Nhia.

"Yeah, an accident," echoed Eli. "It's a good thing that it wasn't your dad's."

My heart sank like a dead battery.

And I don't think I really need to tell you what happened next.

CHAPTER TEN

Facing the Music

my dad is not only a gentleman, but he is *da man*, which is a lot like being *da dad*, which means he can handle quite a lot.

He can eat wasabi without crying.

He can watch a scary movie without flinching.

He can carry a big heavy rock straight across the yard and set it right where my mom wants it.

And he can carry it back again if my mom changes her mind.

When he's had a bad day, my dad can play the piano like crazy until he is his old self again . . . or if he's had a truly horrible day, he can curse a wild blue streak like William Shakespeare.

"Sorrow on thee, thou spongy onion-eyed hugger-mugger!" my dad might say. Then he'd write it down. Or "Clean thine ears, thou lump-ish bum-bailey!" Every time he thinks of a new curse, he writes it on a little piece of paper and puts it in a tin. Cursing like Shakespeare always makes him feel better.

That's my dad. He's *da man*. He can handle just about anything.

So right after school, I put Johnny Astro back where it belonged.

And I slipped in between Calvin and Ani-belly, where I belonged, and we waited with Lucy by the window for our dad to come home.

"Are you *sure* Dad said it was yours?" asked Calvin.

"Maybe we should just have your funeral now," Anibelly whispered sadly.

But I was in luck. When our dad finally stepped through the door, he was in an unusually cheerful mood.

"Hi, everyone!" he said cheerfully.

Silence.

"What's up?"

Silence.

"How 'bout some more fun with Johnny Astro today?"

No one said anything. My dad whistled across the living room. Cheerfully, he reached for Johnny Astro.

Cheerfully, Johnny Astro came down. "Really Flies," said the box. ". . . FLY YOUR SPACE CRAFT ANYWHERE."

Then my dad opened the box.

His whistling stopped.

His breathing stopped.

His feet stopped.

Then he staggered backward.

"WHAAAAAAAAAAT IS THIS?" he wailed. "Johnny Astro, what happened to you?" he cried.

Then he really cried. He put his head in his
hands, and his shoulders went up and down.

Carefully, I put my arm around my dad. Crying is really great. Everything is better afterward. Usually. But this was not usual. This was the best toy ever made.

"WHAT BOOTLESS TOAD-SPOTTED BLADDER DID THIS?" my dad howled. "I'LL SEE THEE HANG'D!"

Gulp.

"WHAT HAPPENED TO MY JOHNNY ASTRO?" he screeched.

And my mom rushed in to see what was going on.

"ALVIN?" my dad bellowed.

My chin quivered. My face wrinkled.

"Dear, you know Alvin can't speak when he's frightened," my mom said calmly.

"This isn't about speaking," my dad said. His teeth were clenched. "It's about respecting other people's things!"

I wanted to cry. But I couldn't. I had to save it for when things got really rough, which I could see was coming faster than a meteorite falling from the sky and aiming straight for me.

"Maybe it was an accident," squeaked Ani-belly.

"An ACCIDENT?" howled my dad. "How can an accident happen on the TOP shelf?"

"Maybe he needed a good show-and-tell," said Calvin. "And the accident happened on the bus."

"WHAAAAAAAT?" roared my dad.

It was time. I began to cry. Crying is really great, it is a good way of softening the blow coming to you. And it helps if the tears run off your chin and you slobber a little and your eyes get puffy and you are a real mess.

"Oh, Alvin, you poor thing," said my mom, which really helps too. She put her arms around me. If lightning struck, it would hit her first, which is probably one of the rules of being a mom.

"This is more than an accident," said my dad. He held up the newly repaired and heavily bandaged Johnny Astro.

"Maybe the guys tried to fix it at recess," said Calvin.

My dad turned seaweed green.

Then he turned sea-foamy.

Then he turned pomegranate, then grapefruit, then orange. Normally I like orange. It is the color of tigers and sherbet and sunsets and mango. But I did not like this orange. It was danger-alert orange, which is only helpful around construction sites.

Anibelly and Calvin stared with their mouths wide open. Getting busted is the best spectator sport around our house, except when you're the one getting busted.

"My Johnny Astro . . . ," my dad wailed. He put the cover back on it and hugged the box sadly. Then he marched off to the piano, like he always does when he's had a hard day, and played like a wild savage beast.

My dad learned to play the piano when he was about my age. So now when he plays, he sounds like Brahms even though his fingers are as thick as bratwurst. As long as he was playing I was okay. And the longer he played, the more okay I was going to be, because as we all know, music is medicine. The more you take, the better you feel.

Finally he stopped. "Alvin needs piano

lessons," said my dad. "It will keep him busy. It will give him confidence. It will change his life."

My dad paused. "It might even give him a good show-and-tell," he added.

And so it was decided that I would take piano lessons, which was really marvelous! I was expecting a grounding, but instead, I was going to face the music.

"Thanks, Dad!" I cried.

My dad said nothing.

I wanted to say something else, something that would make my dad feel good for taking it easy on me. But I didn't know what else to say . . . until I thought of something.

"Someday when I'm old and beastly and have sausages for fingers, I will play the piano just like you, Dad, instead of punishing my kid for destroying my Johnny Astro."

Hair grew on the backs of my dad's hands. He looked strangely beastly again. I think he needed more music to smooth his soul.

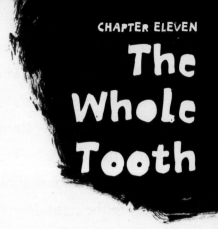

piano lessons were a splendid idea except that every Wednesday after school, when I could have been doing something really useful like taking a bath or vacuuming my room or sharing my sticks and toys with Anibelly, I was to go to Miss Emily's house—alone, without Lucy, without Anibelly, and worst of all, without my Firecracker Man gear or PDK. I might as well have been completely naked!

Now, Miss Emily was no ordinary piano

teacher. She lived at the very end of the street where the trees hang low.

And the grass grows tall.

And shadows stretch like inky tentacles across the road.

And her house looks like a face that sags sadly to the right.

"Go straight to Miss Emily's," my mom said. "She's expecting you. Don't stop anywhere."

I might not have had a problem going to Miss Emily's—that is, if we lived in a normal town. But we do not. A lot of famous dead people live here. And when you are famous, you don't get buried like a regular person under a stone that has your name and telephone number on it. You have to stay in your house to give tours.

The way to know where a famous dead person lives is to look for a sign on their front lawn that says it is their house. For example, at the other end of our street, away from the end where Miss Emily lives, there is a big white house with a sign that says "The House of Ralph Waldo Emerson." Mr. Emerson was famous for writing essays, which is to say he got famous for doing a lot of English homework.

Mr. Emerson died a long time ago, but he still lives in that house. On Thursdays he sweeps his walk. It is very creepy. But his is not the only house like that. There's the "Orchard House, Home of the Alcotts," where Louisa May Alcott leads tours and shows where she used to write stories at a small desk. I've taken the tour with my family. She is definitely a dead author still in her house.

"Calm down," my mom said when we were in Orchard House. "She's an actress dressed up as the author."

I don't think so. It wasn't a show at all. It was for *real*. You could just tell that she had always lived in that house. And her next-door neighbor, Nathaniel Hawthorne, who was also famous for writing stories, is another dead author still in his house. He has a sign outside that says "Wayside." We didn't make it over there after touring Orchard House that day on account of I was scared so stiff I had to be carried home.

So in a normal town I would not have a problem going to Miss Emily's. But this town is not normal.

And Miss Emily's house is not normal. There is a sign on her front lawn. So halfway there, I stopped dead in my tracks. I couldn't bear to get any closer.

"Boo!" said a voice.

"AAAAAAAAAIEEEEEEEEEE!" I screamed.

It was Jules. It is hard to go anywhere without

going past Jules's house, as I've mentioned. And Jules was in the bushes out front.

"You going to piano lessons?" asked Jules.

"Maybe."

"Looks like you were headed straight to piano lessons."

"Maybe I am and maybe I'm not," I said.

"No one walks this way except to go to piano lessons," said Jules. "I see 'em coming and I see 'em going. Mostly they come. Only the lucky few ever go."

"What do you mean?"

"I don't really know," said Jules. "There are only rumors."

"What rumors?"

Jules looked down the street both ways, then whispered, "You know the witch with the yummy house who fattened the kids?"

I nodded. I sure hated that witch who fed Hansel and Gretel to fatten them and then tried to shove them into the oven. She was the most evil witch in the world, worse even than the one who gave Snow White the poisoned apple, on account of she had kept Hansel and Gretel in a cage, which, as everyone knows, could mean years of therapy for them.

"Just learn your scales," Jules said. "But don't eat anything if she tries to feed you. You don't like brownies, do you?"

Gulp. Brownies are my weakness.

"Brownies are her specialty," Jules continued. "You're not going to last very long if you like brownies."

I gasped. Then I turned and dashed home.

When I arrived in my yard, I was in luck. Anibelly was digging with my sticks and Lucy was doing yoga ball next to her. Lucy puts a ball on top of her front paws, stretches out in the down-dog position and touches the tip of her nose to the ball. She can hold the pose until the squirrels come home, or until Anibelly is finished digging holes.

"Anibelly," I shouted. "Come with me, and bring Lucy too."

"Okay," said Anibelly. "C'mon, Luce." Anibelly is fantastic. She always comes when I ask and she never questions why until she has figured it all out, which usually takes a while.

"Aren't you supposed to be going to piano lessons?" she asked when we reached Jules's house. Jules was no longer in the bushes.

"I heard there were going to be snacks," I said. "Just thought you might want to come along."

Anibelly stopped. She put her hands on her hips. She put her left foot out like in the Hokey Pokey, which is her favorite dance. Then she looked at me sideways. "Is that the tooth, Alvin Ho, the whole tooth and nothing but the tooth, so you can help God?" she asked.

Anibelly tapped her toe and waited for an answer.

"Okay . . . I'm allergic," I finally coughed.

"Allergic to piano lessons?"

"No. Allergic to the piano teacher."

"Why?" asked Anibelly, puzzled. "Does she have three fingers?"

"Three fingers???!!!!" A piano teacher with three fingers is like an airplane with only one wing! "I thought she was just the witch from 'Hansel and Gretel'!" I cried.

Anibelly gasped. She hated that witch as much as I did.

"What are you going to do?" Anibelly wanted to know.

"There's only one thing *to* do!" I said. "Capture her and tie her up!"

"Hooray!" cried Anibelly. She sprang up and down. Then she did her Hokey Pokey foot again, which was not a good sign. "Then what?" she asked.

"Then we'll . . . we'll . . . we'll figure something out," I said.

Anibelly shook her head. "Take me home, Alvin Ho," she said. "Take me home right now."

"But I need you," I pleaded. "You're good with strangers. They're always nice to you. And they're nicer to me when you're with me."

"You might be Hansel, but I'm no Gretel," said Anibelly. "I'm Anibelly Ho and I dig holes. I don't sit in cages."

Then Anibelly clung to the bushes in front of Jules's house like a tick to flesh. I could not pry her free until I had promised to take her home. So I did. I took her home. Maybe it was the gentleman thing to do, but I don't know. I didn't care. She really was no use anyway, all balled up like that.

"Don't worry," said Anibelly when she was safely back in our yard and had unballed herself. "Just hold your head high and be a gentleman."

A gentleman? I needed to be Firecracker Man! But it was too late. I would never find all the pieces of my costume in time. I was already late. And late is not good if you're a gentleman, I think.

So I turned and headed back toward the witch's creepy old house.

Just as I was passing Jules's house again, something strange ambled out of Miss Emily's house and started coming toward me.

I froze.

It got closer and closer. . . .

My mouth opened, but nothing came out.

"Mr. Ho?" the figure called. "Are you little Master Ho?"

I did not nod. I did not shake. I did not even breathe. I was not Mr. Ho. I was Alvin Ho. Mr. Ho was my dad. And who was *Master* Ho?

"Heavens, child, you look like you've seen a ghost," said the old woman who stopped in front of me. "We all know there are plenty of 'em around here!" she cackled. It was only a little cackle, but it was a cackle, just the same. "I'm Miss Emily. Your mother called and said you were on your way. We were both worried that you had not yet arrived."

She was just as I had imagined. She was about three hundred years old and a half. She bent like a question mark toward the sidewalk and she looked exactly like her pictures in *The Complete Brothers Grimm Fairy Tales, Deluxe Edition*. There was no doubt that this was the very same witch who had fattened Hansel and Gretel and tried to feed them into the fire. She was the most evil witch in the world, and even worse now for being disguised as a piano teacher.

"Come along, sweetie," she said.

Sweetie? I put my foot down, just like Anibelly, in the Hokey Pokey way. I was going nowhere.

But then I caught a whiff of my pohpoh's almond-scented hand lotion, which is very pleasant. Miss Emily smelled exactly like my pohpoh! Strangely, my feet began to move . . . and before I knew it . . . I was following her like her own shadow! If only Anibelly were with me! She would have helped me resist following my nose, which I have no control over.

Soon I was at the place where the trees hang low.

And the grass grows tall.

And shadows spill like ink across the road.

We floated past the sign in Miss Emily's yard that I couldn't read because we were moving too fast. Then we went right into the mouth of the house that sags sadly to the right.

Inside, it was a dark and stormy night.

A painting of a young woman sitting at a piano stared straight at me.

An enormous white head of Beethoven with blank eyes scowled angrily from a corner.

A plate of brownies sat obediently on the coffee table, a glass of milk beside it.

My eyes moved from the painting to Beethoven to the brownies. Then they stayed on the brownies, which were perfectly dusted with the kind of sugar that looks like fresh-fallen snow. My mouth watered.

"Would you like a snack before we begin?" Miss Emily read my mind. "I made my special

brownies. Quadruple fudge . . . they're still warm
from the oven."

Oven?

Gulp.

"Just learn your scales," Jules's voice echoed inside my ears. "But don't eat anything."

I stepped back. Then I tripped and fell over the piano bench.

"Oh dear," cackled Miss Emily. It was only a little cackle, but it was a witchy kind of cackle just the same.

I was speechless. I didn't know what to say. If I had known that taking my dad's Johnny Astro would end me up in such trouble, I *never* would have taken it.

"Let me help you up," said Miss Emily. Her bony hand and crooked fingers stretched toward me . . . closer . . . and closer . . . until . . . I could see—she only had three fingers!

I can't tell you what my lesson was like after that on account of there was no lesson.

I was completely frozen, like a piece of sausage off a truck.

CHAPTER TWELVE

PSYCHOtherapy

no one can explain why I can't talk in school and now at piano lessons, so once a month, after school, my mom drives me to see a children's psychotherapist to get to the bottom of it.

A therapist is a very smart person who wears glasses and can help you with your problems by asking a lot of questions instead of giving you shots, which is really amazing. But a psycho, as everyone knows, is a crazy person in the movies that you never want to run into in real life. So a *psycho*therapist is a very smart crazy person that you should stay away from for your own good.

I tried to explain this to my mother, but I can never get the words out on account of it's hard to talk about scary things. So I have to outsmart the psycho on my own. It's not easy, but I had it figured out.

ALViN HO'S PSyCHO SURViVAL RULES

1. Carry your PDK.

2. Never volunteer any information.

3. Never look her in the eye.

4. But keep an eye on her.

5. Expect the unexpected.

6. Escape at the first chance.

7. Have a Plan B.

So when my mom dropped me off, I was ready.

"Did you have a good day in school today?" the psycho asked.

I avoided all eye contact.

"Do anything special?"

I kept my hands in plain sight.

"Working on your pitching?"

I nodded. I am always pitching and catching with my gunggung.

"That's good," said the psycho. "I bet you're terrific."

I nodded again.

"How are the piano lessons going?"

Silence.

"Read any good books lately?"

I nodded. I had read a bunch of great books with my dad. We love true tales of courage and accounts of dangerous expeditions. *Tenzing Norgay and the Sherpas of Everest* was especially exciting.

"How's Lucy?"

It was a trick question. There is always so much to tell about my dog. But I caught myself. I've never said a word in therapy. It is too scary. What do you say to a *psycho*?

The clock on the wall clicked *tick, tick, tick*.

Outside, cars swooshed by in the rain.

The psycho sighed.

She shuffled some papers.

"Want to play cards?" she finally asked.

Usually, playing cards is okay. When she runs out of questions, the cards come out and it means the therapy part is over, and when it's over, it's over, and it is just me and the psycho . . . alone . . . with nothing to do . . . but play cards . . . and wait for my mom or dad to pick me up . . . *tick, tick, tick*.

Psychos sure can shuffle. *Flip, flip, flip.*

But she doesn't play very well. She talks too much.

"Making friends is tough, isn't it?" she jabbered.

I held my cards.

"Making friends is hard for grown-ups too," she went on. "So I know how you feel."

I did not move.

"Do you sometimes want to play with kids who don't want to play with you?" she asked.

I nodded. Then I won the first hand.

Shuffle, shuffle. Deal, deal.

"We can't make people play with us who don't want to," said the psycho.

Then I won the second hand. It was too easy. She wasn't paying any attention to her cards.

Then I won the third hand. "But there's always someone great to play with," the psycho jabbered on, "who is also looking for a friend."

The longer we played, the more I won . . . and the more she lost. But she didn't just *lose,* she hardly even looked at her cards! If I played like that, Calvin would have a few unsavory names for me.

"Wipe thy ugly face, thou weedy earth-vexing whey-face," Calvin would say. "Methinks you stink, thou pribbling beetle-headed harpy."

The psycho stopped. "What?" she said. "What did you say?"

Oops. Did I say something?

I kept my eyes low. I kept my hands in plain sight.

"I had no idea you knew Shakespeare." She sounded surprised.

I was surprised too. I didn't know Shakespeare. Shakespeare lived a long time ago. Now he's dead. How could she think I knew him?

"Why, that's really wonderful!" she continued.

But it wasn't wonderful. I hadn't meant to say anything at all. It had just sort of *slipped.*

"I don't know Shakespeare very well," the psycho went on, "but I'm *thrilled* that you can express yourself in that way."

"Sit thee on a spit," I muttered, "then eat my sneakers, thou droning beef-witted nut hook."

Oops. I couldn't stop myself! That's the problem with cursing. Once you start, it's hard to stop.

"Grow unsightly warts, thou half-faced hornbeast!"

"Bathe thyself, thou reeky reeling-ripe pigeon egg!"

The psycho gasped. The look on her face said she didn't think it was so wonderful anymore.

So I made a break for it.

I bolted from my poker hand and ran as fast as I could.

Unfortunately, the psycho was even faster.

She nabbed me as I got to the stairs.

So I let her have it.

"Away, I say, thou currish milk-livered moldwarp!

"Get thee gone, thou beshibbering onion-eyed flap-dragon!

"THY MOTHER WEARS ARMOR!"

CHAPTER THIRTEEN

Rule No. 2

my dad arrived just in the nick of time. If he had been a minute later, I would have gone to Plan B, and who knows how scary that might have been!

My dad did not scream.

He did not yell.

He did not turn eggplant or edamame or Chinese radish or danger-alert orange.

He was not pleased with the psychotherapist's report, but he did not bust me either.

Louise headed for home, making all right-

hand turns because she cannot turn left anymore. She has AA, Automotive Arthritis, she is that old.

And I knew I was headed for trouble. I was thinking of getting a head start on all the crying and wailing I needed to do to soften the blow coming to me, when Louise made a couple of unexpected right turns and before I knew it, she had pulled right in front of Brigham's Ice Cream!

"Did you take a wrong turn?" I squeaked from the backseat. Usually we go to Brigham's to celebrate a birthday or a good report card, but never before for cursing a grown-up.

"No, son," my dad said. I love it when he calls me that. I like it even more than my own name, which I like a lot.

"Then why are we here?" I asked.

"Therapy is rough, right?"

I nodded.

"I had a rough day too," said my dad.

I held my breath.

"So we need to stick together," my dad went on, "and we need some ice cream."

"Oh?" I said. The last time I didn't get the punishment coming to me, I ended up with something worse . . . *way* worse.

"You mean I'm not getting busted?" I asked.

"No, son," said my dad. Normally, I love it when he calls me that. But this was not normal.

Inside, my dad and I walked past other children eating ice cream with their parents. We scooted into a booth.

Tears streamed down my cheeks.

"Waaaaaaaaaaaaaaaaaaaaaaaaaaaaaaaaaaaah!" I wailed, just in case. Our waitress stepped back.

Then I wailed some more. After that I felt much better.

The Triple Monkey Triple Fudge with whipped cream and cherries on top helped too.

But my dad was the most helpful of all.

We had a heart-to-heart, man-to-man talk, just between me and my dad. And this is what I discovered . . .

1. My dad tries to be kind to everyone.
2. He loves superheroes.
3. But he wouldn't rather be one.
4. He'd rather be my dad than anything else in the whole universe.

5. If he could change anything about himself, it might be his bald spot, maybe.
6. If he could change anything about me, it would be nothing.
7. He didn't have a friend until he traded someone a Carl Yastrzemski Rookie for a Hank Aaron Rookie.
8. After that they were best friends.
9. His wish for me is to find a good friend.
10. His second wish for me is that I'd enjoy Shakespearean curses only for fun, not for insulting someone.

"Son," said my dad. "I know it's frustrating and change comes very slowly, but you're making good progress in your therapy."

Then my dad explained that while Rule No. 1 of being a gentleman is no hitting, Rule No. 2 is no cursing or insulting.

"Not at all?" I asked.

"Not one word," he said. Then my dad stood up and puffed out his chest. He looked ten feet tall. My dad is amazing.

I stood up. I puffed out my chest. I did not look ten feet tall. I didn't even look half that size. But it was okay.

"Ready, son?" he said.

"Ready, Dad."

Then I put my arm around him and we went home.

It was the best time I ever had with my dad.

CHAPTER FOURTEEN

The Apes of Math

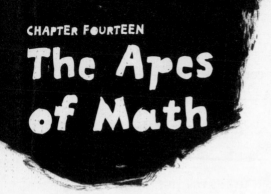

i was making great progress. I could finally remember some things about being a gentleman:

> HOW TO BE a GENTLEMAN
> 1. No hitting.
> 2. No insulting.
> 3. No making anyone cry, even if she is a girl who has only one eye.
>
> 4. Apologize if you break RULE No. 3.
> 5. Don't duke it back (see RULE No. 1).
> 6. Lend a scratching hand to someone with pox.
> 7. Take care of your things.

I could hardly believe it! Suddenly I was closer to being a gentleman! But I was not any closer to having friends.

Fortunately, I remembered that I had some good advice about that from Calvin. It was right there in my PDK:

CALVIN'S RULES FOR Making FRIENDS
1. Say HELLO.
2. JUST say heLLO.
3. tRADe baseball carDS.
4. Trade MORE BaSeBall CARdS.
5. JUST trade Baseball CARdS.

The list was useless . . . until I crossed off:

~~1. Say hello.~~
~~2. Just say hello.~~

Now it was perfect! And since the advice had come from Calvin, I was sure that he meant *his* baseball cards, on account of I didn't have any. And because he didn't write his name on his baseball cards, it could only mean one thing . . . but I asked anyway.

"Calvin," I said, "could I borrow a couple of your *best* cards?"

Srrrrr, srrrr, said Calvin. It was late and he was fast asleep. I should have been asleep too, but I am often up with my flashlight, reading or making lists, because I am afraid of the dark. It's a great time to talk to Calvin on account of he is always pretty agreeable, not like he is during the day, and it certainly sounded like Calvin said "Sure, sure."

• • • •

The next day, I gave the Hank Aaron Rookie to Pinky.

He said nothing.

Then I gave him the Carl Yastrzemski Rookie.

He said nothing.

Then I had nothing else to give.

"Man," Pinky finally said. He stuffed the trading cards into his back pocket and walked away.

Then slowly, my life began to change . . . at recess, Pinky kicked the soccer ball past where I was standing. It was fantastic!

Then during library time, Pinky grabbed Sam's book, so Sam grabbed it back. Then Pinky took it again, so Sam kicked him, which made Nhia jump on Pinky. All this happened right in front of me, between the shelves on earthquakes and volcanoes and the shelves on bats and whales. If I had poked out my arm I could have gotten it broken in several places, which is practically an invitation to jump right in, which I would have done if the librarian hadn't leaped first.

Then in math class, we got a worksheet on the cost of Henry David Thoreau's house:

How much did Henry's house cost?	
Boards	$ 8.03+
Used shingles	4.00
Laths	1.25
Two second-hand windows	2.43
One thousand old bricks	4.00
Two casks of lime	2.40
Hair	0.31
Mantle-tree iron	0.15
Nails	3.90
Hinges and screws	0.14
Latch	0.10
Chalk	0.01
Transportation	1.40
TOTAL	$ 28.12 +

Math is okay. I don't have to read anything out loud. No one holds their breath to see if I am going to take my turn or pass.

The first question asked "What material cost Henry the least?" That was easy.

Next, "How many bricks did Henry buy?" That was easy too.

"Pssssst," hissed Pinky. "What's the answer?" I was on his radar again! I could hardly believe it! My dad and Calvin were right. Baseball cards really do work!

Pinky leaned over and copied my answers onto his paper. Not only was I on Pinky's radar,

but all my answers were on his paper too! Then he motioned for Eli to copy his paper. Then Scooter leaned over and copied from Eli.

"Ahem," said Flea. Flea has only one eye, which is okay, but unfortunately, that eye sees everything, which is annoying. "Cheaters are losers," she said disapprovingly.

"Cyclops are losers," Pinky hissed back.

Flea gasped.

"Fauntleroy," said Miss P. That's Pinky's real name, Fauntleroy, but no one ever calls him that except for grown-ups. "Would you please come up to the board and answer the first question?"

Pinky went up and wrote his answer, *my* answer.

"That's very good, Fauntleroy," said Miss P. "You're getting quicker and better at math."

Pinky beamed. Then he sat down.

Flea gave him The Eye.

Then Eli took his turn. And Miss P said he did a fine job.

But when he got back to his seat, he got The Eye too.

Next Scooter got his turn. And Miss P said he was great. Normally, he is not great in math, numbers are a mystery to him. He got The Eye.

Then before I knew it, math class was over.

In fact, school was over.

And I never got my turn! Only the apes of math got turns. It was not fair! I was as mad as a salmon swimming upstream.

And so was Flea. Her eye was big and round. "It's really not fair you didn't get your turn," said Flea as we were leaving.

I nodded.

"After all, they were all *your* answers," she added, just as we passed Miss P standing in the doorway saying good-bye to everyone. I was really glad that Flea let Miss P know.

Then we got on the bus.

"Hey, buddy," Pinky said when I sat down.

Buddy? He was calling me buddy?

"You're okay," said Pinky, sitting down next to me. "But you gotta get rid of that girlfriend of yours." He laughed and pointed at Flea, who had sat down in the seat in front of me.

I shrank. I knew that Flea took no nonsense. But Pinky didn't know. He was *this* close to taking an uppercut from her.

"Maybe you could play with us sometime," said Pinky.

"Really?" I could hardly wait.

The wheels on the bus went round and round. We bounced up and down.

"But . . . you'll have to do a few things first," said Pinky.

"Like what?" I asked.

"I'll let you know," said Pinky.

"Does everyone have to do them?" I asked.

"Just you," said Pinky. "It's a new rule, dude."

I swallowed.

"Okay." I swallowed. "Dude."

CHAPTER FIFTEEN

The Problem With Joining a Gang

the first problem with joining a gang is that the pressure starts right away.

"I dare you to stick your tongue out at the bus driver," ordered Pinky. The gang followed us off the bus.

I stood in my driveway. I stuck out my tongue at the bus driver. She didn't look too pleased. But Pinky did.

"I dare you to yell a bad word at the bus," ordered Pinky as the bus pulled away. "Now!"

"ZOUNDS!" I yelled at the top of my lungs.

"What?" asked Eli.

"Behold thy mirror, thou spleeny, knotty-pated dewberry!" I added, for good measure.

"Okay, forget it," said Pinky impatiently. "Whatever."

The second problem with joining a gang is that Flea gave me The Eye, then turned and went down the street, swinging her cool peg leg and all, without a word.

The third problem with joining a gang is that you don't know what they'll make you do . . . but I had a feeling it would be scary. I thought about this as we walked up my driveway.

"I dare you . . . ," said Pinky, looking up, ". . . to jump off the roof of your house!"

"I'm telling Mom," said Calvin, who was right behind us. He ran into the house. "Mo-o-o-om!" I heard him yell. "Mo-o-o-om!"

My heart thumped like crazy. My mom is an ace rescuer. She would save me. She always does.

But my mom did not come out. And neither did Calvin.

So I scratched the old pox on my left side. Then I scratched the old pox on my right side. Then I looked up at the roof of my house. It was a long way up. I swallowed. It was all I could do not to cry. But it is important at moments like this to not show how you really feel. It is like playing poker. Even if you're losing, you have to pretend you're winning.

"Well?" said Pinky.

"Okay," I said. But I was not okay. I could just about pee in my pants! One moment I am standing in my driveway, the next moment I could be *on* my driveway, *dead*, just like that.

"Well?" said Pinky. "What are you waiting for?"

"I gotta use the bathroom first," I said. I ran inside, rushed up the stairs and used the bathroom.

Then I went into my bedroom and looked out the window.

It was a long way down.

Calvin and Anibelly were playing catch with GungGung in the backyard. Farther down the road, Flea was playing by herself in her own backyard, building something that looked like a pyramid. It was fabulous, even from far away.

"This is a fastball." GungGung's voice floated up into my ears. He is my grandpa from my mom's side. When he is at my house after school, it means that my mom is at work and he is here to keep his eye on things.

I looked down at Pinky. He was shouting something at me and his face was very pink. He looked *much* smaller than he used to. In fact, from where I was, Pinky was just a pinky!

I went back downstairs.

"I'm not going to jump off my roof," I told Pinky.

"Why not?"

"I have acrophobia," I said.

"Huh?" said Pinky.

"Fear of heights," I explained.

"Well, then . . . ," said Pinky. "I dare you . . . to . . . watch a scary movie!"

I froze. I hate scary movies. They give me nightmares. After I watch one, I can't eat, I can't talk, I can't walk, I can't sleep, I can't get it out of my head. But I supposed it was better than jumping to my death in my own driveway and then having Louise run over my dead body.

I wanted to cry like the end of a rain pipe on a rainy day. But I didn't. It is important at moments like this to not show how you really feel. It is like marching to the doctor's office for a vaccination. Even though the shot could kill you, you still have to look like you don't know it.

So I began to march.

Fortunately, the longest path to the TV at our house is through the backyard.

"Hi, Alvin!" called Anibelly cheerfully. She is always happy to see me, especially after school. "Was that you cursing like an infectious, pox-marked measle at the school bus?"

I didn't answer. Anibelly was wearing *my* mitt, the one with *my* name on it. And she was throwing *my* ball, the one that used to belong to Daisuke Matsuzaka, with her two fingers together on top. She snapped the ball into GungGung's glove. *Ffffppht.* It was a fastball, all right, but it really wasn't that fast. She was just *pretending* it was fast.

But the *sound* of Anibelly's fastball smacking into the mitt is a little scary. It stopped the gang dead in their tracks.

"You want to throw, Alvin?" asked Anibelly. "I'll catch."

"No thanks," I lied. "I've got something better to do."

"Like what?"

"Like prove his bravery," said Pinky, "so that he can play with us at school."

Anibelly narrowed her eyes. She put out her Hokey Pokey foot and made a face that said they were going to have to deal with her first.

"Anibelly," said GungGung. "If Alvin would rather not play catch, it's okay."

My gunggung loves baseball. He is an ace pitching machine. And playing catch with him is our favorite thing to do after school whenever he is around. So Anibelly and GungGung went back to throwing the ball and the gang and I stood there and watched.

"This is a knuckleball," GungGung said, showing Anibelly and Calvin. He bent his two fingers at the knuckles so that they came up like two rabbit ears on the ball, and pitched it to Calvin. *Ffffslurrruuullluuurpf.* It was slow and tricky. Calvin hardly knew where it was going!

"This is a changeup," said my gunggung. He shifted his middle finger and fourth finger to grip the ball from the top, with the index finger

and pinky gripping from the sides and the thumb on the bottom, and snapped it into Ani-belly's glove. *Ummmmph*. It looked like a fastball but was a bit slower. Another tricky ball. It can fool you into swinging early.

Then my gunggung demonstrated the two-seam fastball and the four-seam fastball. Then the split-finger and its cousin, the nastier, slower forkball. They are *baaaad*, meaning they are fantastic!

I could hardly stand it. I love throwing with my gunggung. I love it more than digging holes. And I definitely love it more than doing dares from Pinky. To make matters worse, there was Anibelly using my glove and ball!

"I thought you boys had something better to do," said GungGung.

No one moved. A breeze swirled crispy leaves up and around our ankles.

"Oh yeah . . . ," said Pinky finally. "We do."

And that is the worst problem with joining a gang. Someone else speaks for you.

CHAPTER SIXTEEN

A Horrific Thing

by the time we came up from the basement after watching *Alien Babies Land from Outer Space*, it was getting dark. The house was very quiet except for the wind weeping and wailing through the walls and the faint machine-gun sound of my mom's sewing machine coming from upstairs. Besides being an ace pitching machine my gunggung also likes to sew.

"That w-w-wasn't a very s-s-scary movie at all," stammered Scooter.

"N-no, it wasn't," said Eli.

"I've s-seen s-s-scarier," said Nhia, shud-dering.

I said nothing.

"Let's go throw some b-balls," said Pinky.

"Okay," said Hobson.

"*Woohoo!*" said Pinky, picking up my ball and glove, which Anibelly had left by the door. "We even have an autographed b-b-baseball by Alvin Ho!"

The gang slapped high fives.

I slapped nothing.

"I think there's s-s-something wrong with Alvin," said Sam.

I could hardly move. I could hardly blink. I could hardly breathe. I could hardly do anything but watch alien babies invade Earth and crawl around like zombies, over and over again in my mind.

But Pinky and the gang had already gone out, and so had my glove and ball. And so I followed, like a zombie myself.

Outside, it was a dark and shadowy night.

The tree reached its crooked fingers toward me. The garden hose slithered and hissed.

Usually, no one pitches at our house when it gets dark. You can't see what you're doing and if you miss, you could have a terrible accident.

"I'd like to learn the forkball," Pinky said to me. "Show me." He threw me the ball and backed up.

I froze. A forkball is a killer. It is slow and nasty. Even in daylight, you can hardly tell where it's going. If Pinky didn't catch it, the ball could smack him right between the eyes.

"C'mon!" said Pinky. "You waitin' for retire-
ment or something?"

I shivered. I squinted. It
was hard to tell the gang
apart from the other creepy
shadows in the yard.

"I haven't got all night!"
screeched Pinky.

So I wound my
pitch, leaned back on
one leg, then fired it with all my
might. . . .

There was no thud in the glove.

A thick, soupy silence poured into our
ears.

Then *CRAAAAAAACK!* The
sound of a window splintering
into a million diamonds.

Oops.

"I think I hear my mom calling," said Pinky. He tossed my
glove and had started across the
yard when . . .

A Horrific Thing emerged from the shadows . . . and came charging toward us. Half of it was green and the other half was black. Scales ran along one side, and warts ran down the other.

I was ready to pee in my pants. But I didn't. At moments like this, it is important to have already used the bathroom, which I had.

"*AAAAAAAAAAAAACK!*" Pinky screamed a belly-button-piercing scream. "*AAAAAAAAAA-AAAAAAAAAAAAAAAAAAAAAAAAAAAACK!*"

The wind howled and hammered at the house. The fence groaned and creaked.

I wanted to scream my head off, but I couldn't. Nothing came out.

My heart stopped.

My breath stopped.

My eyes shut. When I opened them again, I saw that Pinky had—peed in his pants!

I didn't know what to say. And neither did the rest of the gang. What do you say when someone's just embarrassed himself to death?

The Horrific Thing moved closer. "Lalala-lalalalalala," it sang.

Pinky turned and ran. "*AAAAAAAAAAAA-AAAAACK!*" he screamed.

"Hi, Alvin!" said the Horrific Thing. It was Anibelly's voice . . . but it was not Anibelly. "Lalalalalalalala," it sang again.

Had the Horrific Thing swallowed Anibelly?

"Do you like my Halloween costume, Alvin?" said Anibelly's voice. "GungGung just finished it!"

The Horrific Thing twirled menacingly one way and then menacingly the other way. It was uglier than any of the alien babies and scarier than the whole movie from beginning to end.

"Wh-wh-what are you?" I asked.

"Half witch and half dragon," said Anibelly's voice. "I couldn't decide, so GungGung said I could be both!"

"Oh," I said.

Then—surprise, surprise—I remembered to say something nice to Anibelly. "You look terrific!" I said, even though she was ugly enough to make you run.

"You'd better come in now," called my gung-gung from the house. He was a dark shape against the bright light in the doorway. Anibelly and I ran toward the light.

"Lucky your mother wasn't home," my gung-gung said as I stepped past him. "You can tell her what happened in the morning."

I nodded. Then I looked over my shoulder. The rest of the gang had disappeared. Our yard was quiet. The house next door was completely dark and quiet too.

Lucky the neighbors weren't home either.

CHAPTER SEVENTEEN

Death by Volcano

after breakfast the next morning, and after I had forgotten to tell my mom about what had happened with the gang, I dashed over to Pinky's house as quickly as I could. Pinky was still in his pajamas watching cartoons. I was in my Firecracker Man outfit from head to toe. It was Saturday. The world needed saving and there was no time to waste. But first . . . I tapped on his living room window.

"I want a refund," I said when Pinky came to the door.

"What refund?" asked Pinky.

"The Hank Aaron Rookie and the Carl Yastrzemski Rookie," I said. "I want them back."

"But I thought we were friends," said Pinky.

I had thought about it all night, in between reruns of alien babies crawling around inside my head. And this is what I thought: playing with Pinky was not a good trade for the cards.

"I don't like doing the things you do," I said.

"Why not?" asked Pinky.

"I'm just not talented in that way," I said.

Pinky shrugged. "Yeah, you're right," he said. Then he went back into his house. When he came to the door again, he handed over the cards.

The Rookies were okay. There is a good reason why baseball cards are in plastic pockets. It keeps them dry, in case of accidents. I breathed a sigh of relief.

"You sure you want to do this?" Pinky asked.

I nodded. I was very sure.

"If I don't play with you, who will?"

I shrugged. I didn't really know. But I knew I didn't want to play with him.

•–•–•

Flea's house was on the way home. It is not on the way to everywhere, like Jules's house, but it is on the way to some things, some of the time.

And Flea was in her yard, swinging her arms wildly and kicking her peg leg and her regular leg equally wildly. "Ha!" she screamed, chopping her arms through the air. "Ha-ha!" She chopped the other way.

"Hi," I said.

"Ha!" said Flea, kicking the air behind her.

"Whatcha doing?"

"Aggression for Girls," said Flea. "Want to try? It's fun!"

I shrugged. "Okay." I squeezed through a loose board in the fence.

Flea sliced her arm like a sword through the air. She added a kick to the side. It was fabulous! I sliced and kicked too. "Ha!" she screamed again. "Ha-ha!" "Ha!" I copied. "Ha-ha!" We chopped and kicked until we were out of chops and kicks. After that we went inside and watched an action movie with Boatswain. He swam around like crazy during commercials, but he stayed fixed in one spot in his bowl during the action scenes, unblinking, watching the movie. It was the most amazing thing I had ever seen.

"I'll trade you a Carl Yastrzemski Rookie and

a Hank Aaron Rookie for your fish," I said, holding out the cards.

"No way!" said Flea.

"How about the rookies *and* . . . a piece of gum!" I said. I reached into my back pocket, but the gum was not there. Then I remembered that I had traded it to Pinky long ago.

"This fish is not for sale," said Flea. "He's family. Isn't that right, Boatswain?"

Boatswain nodded, I swear it. "Why, how now, putz . . . ," I began in a Shakespearean curse. Then I stopped myself. I cleared my throat.

"I have something to say," I said.

"Okay," said Flea.

I looked around. I didn't really want to say it. It was something hard to say. It was much harder than cursing or insulting.

"Can I try on your eye patch?" I asked.

"Okay," said Flea. She pulled it off and I pulled it on.

I blinked. It was fantastic!

Flea's good eye blinked too. Her other eye looked as soft as a baby's and stayed shut.

"You're blind in that eye?" I asked.

"Yup," said Flea.

"How come?" I asked.

"I come from a long line of pirates," said Flea.

It was just as I'd thought. "Is that how you got a peg leg too?" I asked.

"Yup," said Flea.

I nodded, speechless. Then I gave Flea her eye patch back.

"Was that what you wanted to say?" asked Flea.

I shook my head. It wasn't at all what I had wanted to say. But now I had run out of other things to say. So I had to say it.

"I'msorrythatIdidn'tstickupforyouyesterday-inmathclassandonthebus," I said.

Flea blinked.

Then she blinked again.

I held my breath.

"Okay," she finally said. "I forgive you."

What a relief.

So then I asked the question I'd been dying to ask, "What's that in your backyard?"

"C'mon," she said. "I'll show you." We hurried outside.

And there, in Flea's backyard, in broad daylight—gulp—was a real live VOLCANO! It was HUGE. It was made of mud and dirt and something called chicken wire, but there were no chickens, only wire.

Flea poured a bucket of vinegar and some baking soda into the top and lava bubbled out. It was a MESS! And it was AMAZING!

After the bubbling stopped, it got kind of quiet in the backyard.

Flea looked at me.

And I looked at Flea.

"What are you going to be for Halloween?" I finally asked.

"A princess," said Flea. "I'm always a princess."

"Oh," I said. I didn't like princesses. They are stu . . . I mean silly. Princesses make me sick. And just as I was about to say how much I hate princesses, I heard something else come out of my mouth.

"You'd make a good princess."

Grow unsightly warts! How did I say that?

"Thank you," said Flea. "What are you going to be?"

"A gentleman," I said.

"Oh," said Flea.

It grew kind of quiet again.

Then she remembered her manners.

"You'd make a good one," she said.

"Thanks," I said.

Then we poured more vinegar and baking soda into the volcano. Lava bubbled out like crazy.

"Death by volcano!" I screamed, leaping and jumping over the foamy lava.

"*Rrrrrrrrrrrrrrrrrrrrrrrrrrrrr!*" roared Flea, leaping and jumping like crazy too. There were plastic Minutemen and Redcoats and trucks and motorcycles and packs of ferocious tuojiangosaurus and a flock of velociraptors that we had to save. So we did. It took all afternoon, but we saved them all.

After we finished, Flea brought out her book, *The Book on Alvin*. She drew Firecracker Man saving the world from death and destruction on the side of a volcano. It was really super-duper!

"Do you think we can do this again sometime?" I asked.

"Sure," said Flea. "Anytime."

Anytime. It sounded like something friends say to each other.

And I blasted off toward home.

•••••

"Alvin," said my mother when Firecracker Man blasted into the kitchen.

Uh-oh. The look on her face was not so great.

"Did you put a baseball through the neighbor's window?"

"What baseball?" I asked innocently. "Not I."

"It was in her sink," said my dad. "And it had your name on it, son."

I love it when he calls me that, usually.

Alvin Ho's
Woeful Glossary

Alvin Ho—(1) Aka Firecracker Man, (2) a gentleman-in-training.

American Revolutionary War—Started in Concord, Massachusetts, which is hard to spell. Revolutionaries fired cannons and all sorts of gunshots at the British to get rid of them. It took a long time, from 1775 to 1783, with lots of help from France, Spain and the Netherlands. But in the end, the British went home and the American colonies became a new country.

Anibelly—(1) Messes with my things, (2) eats my food, (3) drinks my chocolate milk, (4) generally gets in my way.

Beethoven—(1) Aka Ludwig van Beethoven, (2) famous German composer, (3) wrote nine symphonies, one violin concerto and lots of hard stuff for the piano, (4) scary-looking.

Boatswain—Pronounced "BO-sun." (1) An officer on a ship in charge of the maintenance of the vessel, (2) the name of Flea's fish.

Brahms—(1) Aka Johannes Brahms, (2) another famous German composer, (3) born six years after Beethoven's death, (4) loved Beethoven's music, (5) kept a marble bust of Beethoven that looked down on him while he composed.

bratwurst—German sausage.

Calvin—(1) Knows everything, (2) owns everything, (3) is quite agreeable late at night.

Carl Yastrzemski—Pronounced "Ya-STREM-ski." Nicknamed Yaz or Captain Carl. Played his amazing entire twenty-three-year career with the Boston Red Sox. He was a left fielder, a first baseman and a star hitter. He is the Red Sox all-time leader in career RBIs, runs, hits, singles, doubles, total bases and games played and is second for home runs, behind Ted Williams. His dad was a potato farmer.

chicken pox—It's just itchy pox. A chicken doesn't come with it.

Chinese radish—A vegetable that looks like a big white carrot.

Concord, Massachusetts—(1) Birthplace of the American Revolution, (2) eighteen miles northwest of Boston, (3) home of famous dead authors (see below), (4) my home, (5) hard to spell.

Daisuke Matsuzaka—Born in Japan in 1980 and nicknamed the Monster in Japan and Dice-K in the United States. K means strikeout! During his first season with the Boston Red Sox in 2007, Dice-K broke the Red Sox rookie record for the most strikeouts in a season, with 156. He finished the season with 201 strikeouts and became the first Japanese pitcher in history to start and win a World Series game.

edamame—Pronounced "ed-a-MA-may." A vegetable that looks like peas in a pod.

feng shui—Pronounced "fung SHWAY." A Chinese way of placing stuff, like houses and furniture and trees and rocks, so that everything looks fantastic!

Flea—(1) A girl, (2) short for Sophie, (3) her grandpa, who couldn't hear very well, thought her parents had said that her name was Flea when she was born.

flybox—(1) Also called a tackle box, in which different flies, plugs, spinners, jigs, spoons, poppers, lures, hooks, lines, bobbers and sinkers are stored for use in fishing, (2) handy for holding a PDK.

Frida Kahlo—Mexico's most famous woman artist. When she was six she had a disease called polio. Her right leg became very thin and the kids at school called her Frida *pato a palo*, or Frida "peg leg."

gung fu—Aka kung fu or gong fu. Chinese exercises that look cool in the movies, but that break things around the house when you go crazy practicing them after watching a gung fu movie.

GungGung—(1) Ace pitching machine, (2) ace costume maker, (3) my mom's dad.

Hank Aaron—(1) Aka Hammer, Hammerin' Hank or Bad Henry, (2) set the Major Baseball League's home run record of 755 in 1976, (3) a 1952 Topps Hank Aaron Rookie card sold for $100,000 in 2000.

Henry David Thoreau—Pronounced "THOR-ow." Famous dead author who loved nature. Built a small cabin in the woods and lived in it for two years before he got tired of it and moved home.

Johnny Astro—A toy that really flies. Invented in the 1960s by toy genius Sol Friedman. Hard to find. Impossible to repair. If you break it, you might as well plan your funeral.

kickboxing—Not real boxing. Involves punching the air while bouncing back and forth in a boxing dance. Usually done in a class at the Y.

kimchi—Pickled cabbage that explodes in your throat and makes you cry.

Louisa May Alcott—Famous dead author who wrote *Little Women*. Wrote at a small desk her father made for her. Lived in the brown house on Lexington Road. Still does.

Minutemen—A small handpicked elite force of the Massachusetts militia, who were "ready in a minute." They were the first to arrive at a battle during the American Revolutionary War.

Nathaniel Hawthorne—Famous dead author who wrote *The Scarlet Letter* and *The House of the Seven Gables* and many short stories. Loved taking walks with his wife, Sophia. Lived next door to Louisa May Alcott. Still does.

Patriots' Day—A holiday commemorating the Battles of Lexington and Concord, the first battles of the American Revolutionary War, fought on April 19, 1775.

Paul Gauguin—Pronounced "goh-GAN." French painter who lived in Peru with his mom for four years from the time he was about Anibelly's age to the time that he was my age. Then he moved back to France. When he was older, he lived in Tahiti and painted the people there, using bright colors. A friend of Vincent van Gogh.

PohPoh—(1) My grandmother on my mother's side, (2) good at rubbing stuff on chicken pox, mosquito bites, bee stings and scraped knees, (3) keeps an eye on GungGung.

psychotherapy—A scary way to help you not be so scared.

Ralph Waldo Emerson—Famous dead author who wrote many essays. Took long walks with his friend Henry David Thoreau. President Abraham Lincoln came to dinner at his home once. Lived in the big white house on Cambridge Turnpike. Still does.

Redcoats—Soldiers of the British Army during the American Revolutionary War. Red was the color of their uniform.

Tenzing Norgay—The first to climb to the top of Mount Everest with Edmund Hillary in May 1953.

tourniquet—A tight band tied around a limb to stop severe bleeding. Used to find a vein for blood donation. Also used in the event of amputation.

Vincent van Gogh—Dutch artist who flunked out of many different jobs before he discovered that he was a painter at age twenty-seven. He liked painting peasants and poor people. When Vincent painted at night, he stuck candles in his hat so that he could see better.

Walden Pond—(1) Looks like a big lake to me, (2) just right for swimming, (3) in the old days, they used to harvest ice here in winter and pack it in hay and put it on a train that took it as far as Chicago, (4) Henry David Thoreau built his cabin here.

wasabi—Pronounced "wa-SAH-be." A green paste made from horseradish that you eat with sushi. Explodes inside your nose and makes you cry.

William Shakespeare—Dead English author. Born after Christopher Columbus discovered the Americas, but died before the British Army wore red. Wrote lots of plays, poems, curses, everything. When he ran out of words, he made up new ones. Never lived in Concord.

yehyeh—Chinese word for grandpop on your father's side.